WRITTEN BY **Victoria Kann** & **Elizabeth Kann**

ILLUSTRATED BY **Victoria Kann**

Purplicious

First published in the US in 2008 by HarperCollins Children's Books.
First published in the UK in 2015 by Hodder Children's Books.

Text copyright © 2008 by Elizabeth Kann and Victoria Kann, Inc.
Illustrations copyright © 2008 by Victoria Kann, Inc.
Pinkalicious and all related logos and characters are
trademarks of Victoria Kann, used with her permission.

Hodder Children's Books, an imprint of Hachette Children's Group
Part of Hodder & Stoughton
Carmelite House, 50 Victoria Embankment, London EC4Y 0DZ

The right of Elizabeth and Victoria Kann to be identified as the authors
and Victoria Kann as the illustrator of this Work has been asserted
by them in accordance with Copyright, Designs and Patents Act 1988.

A catalogue record of this book is available from the British Library.

ISBN: 978 1 444 921625
10 9 8 7 6 5 4 3 2 1

Printed in China

An Hachette UK Company.

www.hachette.co.uk   www.thinkpinkalicious.com   www.facebook.com/pinkalicious

To
Samantha
~E.K.

To
Maria
~V.K.

I was in art class, painting a picture.

"What are you painting?" asked Kendra.

"A picture of a sunset," I said.

"Pinkalicious, why does everything you
paint have to have pink in it?" asked Tara.

"Because pink is my favourite colour,"
I answered.

"Don't you know, the new colour is black. All the girls
like black now," said Brittany.

"Black is in," said Beatrice during playtime.

"Pink is putrid," announced Pauline, while dangling from the monkey bars.

"Yeah, pink stinks!" added Sophia.

On the bus ride home from
school, no one would sit with me.

"Pink is for babies and little girls. We aren't going
to be friends with a baaaby," taunted Tiffany.

"You don't have to be a baby or a little girl to like the colour
pink. Pink is for everyone," I said. "Even my brother likes pink."

"How funny! A boy who likes pink?!" everyone laughed.
"Isn't it time you moved *beyond* pink?"

After school no one would play princesses with me. I went to my room and counted all my pink things. I had a pink crayon, a pink piggy bank, a pink tiara, even a giant pink bunny. I had more than a hundred pink possessions. The only black thing I had was an ugly plastic spider left over from Halloween.

I wrote with my pink
pen in my pink diary:

Tuesday

I am who I am and I like pink.

That week, after the girls teased me in school, I wrote in my diary every day. Then I cried into my pink hankie.

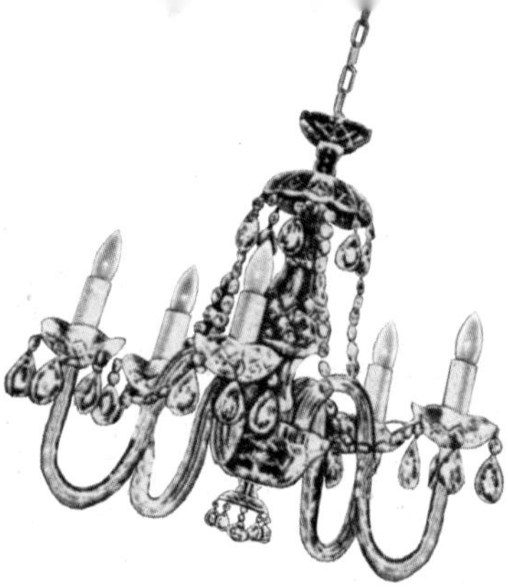

Wednesday

Pink makes
me happy
but mean
girls make
me sad.

Friday

Pink
has no
purpose.

Thursday

Pink is
a lonely
Colour.

On Saturday, Mummy, Daddy, Peter and
I went to get ice cream to cheer me up.

"Pinkalicious, what would you like?" asked Mr Swizzle. "Magenta Mint Mango, or perhaps you would enjoy Pink Passion Fruit Paradise?"

"No thanks. I'll just have... um... Vanilla."

I sighed, looking around to see who might see me from my school.

"How about you, Peter? Would you like your usual, Plum Pink Perfection?"

"Yes! Yes, thank you!"
said Peter.

"Pink ice cream
is for babies!"
I said to Peter.

"Pinkalicious, aren't you going to eat your
ice cream?" asked Mummy.

"Well, I'm actually not that hungry."
The ice cream tasted bland to me.
I couldn't possibly eat it.

"Pinkalicious has the blues," Daddy said that night when I wouldn't play pink-pong with him.

"What does it mean when you have the blues?" I said.

"It means that you feel sad. Why do you feel sad?"

"No one will play with me because I like the colour pink. All the girls like the colour black now and I don't."

"Are you sure *all* the girls like black? Maybe there are other kids who like pink."

"Everyone hates pink. You don't know anything!"
I shouted, running to my room.

"I'm the only one in
the whole wide world
who likes pink. I am
all alone. No one
understands me,"
I said to myself.

On Monday I noticed a girl in art class.
She was painting a beautiful picture.

"What are you painting?" I asked.

"It's a picture of a cake, but the blue icing doesn't look right.
I think I need some pink, and then it will be perfect."

"Really?" I asked. "You *like* pink?
Don't you think pink is for babies?"

"Pink is perfect," she answered.
"Watch this and you'll
see why..."

She mixed the pink paint into the blue, and the icing turned purple. "Pink is powerful," she said. "Look, it turned blue into purple."

"Purple is pretty," I said.

"Not just pretty... it's purplicious!"